MR. DUCK MEANS BUSINESS

TAMMI SAUER

A Paula Wiseman Book
Simon & Schuster Books for Young Readers
New York London Toronto Sydney

ILLUSTRATED BY
JEFF MACK

For Cynthea Liu, who always means business
—T. S.

For Broccoli Kallock
—J. M.

SIMON & SCHUSTER BOOKS FOR YOUNG READERS
An imprint of Simon & Schuster Children's Publishing Division · 1230 Avenue of the Americas, New York, New York 10020
Text copyright © 2011 by Tammi Sauer · Illustrations copyright © 2011 by Jeff Mack

For information about special discounts for bulk purchases, please contact Simon & Schuster Special Sales at 1-866-506-1949 or business@simonandschuster.com.
The Simon & Schuster Speakers Bureau can bring authors to your live event. For more information or to book an event, contact
the Simon & Schuster Speakers Bureau at 1-866-248-3049 or visit our website at www.simonspeakers.com.
Book design by Lucy Ruth Cummins · The text for this book is set in Graham.
The illustrations for this book are rendered in acrylic.
Manufactured in the United States of America · 0211 PCR
2 4 6 8 10 9 7 5 3
Library of Congress Cataloging-in-Publication Data
Sauer, Tammi. Mr. Duck means business / Tammi Sauer ; illustrated by Jeff Mack.—1st ed. p. cm.
"A Paula Wiseman Book."
Summary: Mr. Duck enjoys a quiet morning routine on his private pond every day until other animals mistakenly think he has invited them to join him.
ISBN 978-1-4169-8522-8 (hardcover) [1. Ducks—Fiction. 2. Domestic animals—Fiction. 3. Ponds—Fiction.
4. Humorous stories.] I. Mack, Jeff, ill. II. Title.
PZ7.S2502 Mr 2011
[E]—dc22
2009047248

Mr. Duck lived by himself at the pond.
Each day he followed a tight schedule.

From 6:00 in the morning until 7:00, he would stretch his wings.

From 7:00 until 8:00, he would fluff his feathers.

At precisely 8:01, he would glide across the perfectly still water.

"Ah," said Mr. Duck. "It's so peaceful. So quiet. I have everything I need."

Day after day, week after week, and year after year, everything was the same.

And Mr. Duck was very happy.

Then one especially hot summer day, Mr. Duck had just begun his morning gliding when he saw . . .

Pig?

Mr. Duck sputtered.

He muttered.

He tail-a-fluttered.

But Pig did *not* get the message.

Mr. Duck was all set to give Pig a strongly worded speech regarding private property when . . .

"Well, there you are," said Cow.
"Let's see your moooves," called
Pig. "Jump in!"
"You don't mind, do you, Mr. Duck?"
said Cow as she
plowed past.

"Moo, mooooo."
SPLASH!

Mr. Duck grumbled.

He mumbled.

He flip-flop-fumbled.

But Pig and Cow did *not* get the message.

Mr. Duck was all set to tell them what's what when . . .

"Hey!" said Goat. "We've been looking all over for you!"

"Anyone up for a game of Marco Polo?" called Pig.

"Last one in is a rotten egg!" cheeped a chick.

"C'mon, Mr. Duck!" said Cow. "You're it!"

The water got wild. The scenery got crowded.
And the peace and quiet?

It.
Was.
Gone.

Mr. Duck tapped.

He flapped.

He totally SNAPPED.

"QUA-A-A-A-A-ACKKK!"

And somebody got the message.

"Perhaps we've overstayed our welcome," said Chick.

"*Oh*," said the other animals.

"Out! Out! Out of *my* pond!" cried Mr. Duck.

"This time I mean business!"

"So sorry."

"My apologies."

"Good-bye for GOOD!" said Mr. Duck.

"Sorry to have bothered you," said Chick.
"Thanks for letting us swim in your pond."

Alone at last, Mr. Duck returned to his routine.

He stretched his wings.

There was no splashy belly flopping.

He fluffed his feathers.

There was no annoying water ballet.

He glided across the perfectly still water.

There was certainly no rowdy round of Marco Polo.

"Ah," said Mr. Duck. "It's so peaceful. So quiet. And that's just the way I like it!"

On Monday:
Quiet.

On Tuesday:
Very quiet.

On Wednesday:
Peaceful.

On Thursday:
Very peaceful.

On Friday:
YAWWWWNNN.

On Saturday:
Mr. Duck twiddled his feathers. Peacefully and quietly, of course.

And on Sunday?

Mr. Duck had a plan!

These days Mr. Duck
still loves to stretch at
6:00.

He still loves to fluff his
feathers at 7:00.

He still loves to glide across the perfectly still water at precisely 8:01.

But sometimes life calls for a little noise . . .

especially with friends.